THIS CANDLEWICK BOOK BELONGS TO:

For
Emily, Sophie, Felix, and Ben

New U.S. paperback edition 2003

First published in Great Britain in 1985 by Walker Books Ltd., London.

The Library of Congress has cataloged the first U.S. paperback edition as follows:

Craig, Helen.
Susie and Alfred in the night of the paper bag monsters /
Helen Craig. — 1st U.S. paperback ed.
"First published in Great Britain in 1985 by Walker Books Ltd., London" — T.p. verso.
Summary: Pig friends Susie and Alfred quarrel while preparing for
a costume party but make up in time to go together as scary paper bag monsters.
ISBN 1-56402-120-3
[1. Pigs—Fiction. 2. Costume—Fiction. 3. Parties—Fiction.]
I. Title. II. Title: Night of the paper bag monsters.
PZ7.C84418Surr   1994
[E]—dc20   92-44610
New U.S. paperback edition ISBN 0-7636-2037-8

2 4 6 8 10 9 7 5 3 1

Printed in China

The illustrations in this book were done in pen and watercolor.

Candlewick Press
2067 Massachusetts Avenue
Cambridge, Massachusetts 02140

visit us at www.candlewick.com

SUSIE AND ALFRED

· IN ·

❖ **THE NIGHT OF THE PAPER BAG MONSTERS** ❖

· HELEN CRAIG ·

CANDLEWICK PRESS
CAMBRIDGE, MASSACHUSETTS

Susie was spending the day with Alfred.
He was worried. "We have to think of something
to wear to the costume party tonight," he said.
"Should we go as ghosts?" suggested Susie.

"*Whooo, whooo, whooo!*" howled the ghosts.
"Hello, Susie! Hello, Alfred!
 Having fun?" asked Alfred's mother.

"This is no good," complained Alfred. "We have to do something so different that no one will recognize us."

In the garden shed they found
some very strong paper bags.

"Grrr, grrr, grrr!" growled Alfred. "I'm a terrible monster!"
"No, you're not," said Susie. "You're a pig in a
brown paper bag!"

"Let's paint faces on the bags then," said Alfred,
    and they got to work.

Everything was going very well until Alfred stepped
back to admire his work. He accidentally knocked
a can of green paint all over Susie's paper bag.

"Oh, you creep!" cried Susie. "You ruined all
my work!" She picked up the can of red paint
and poured it over Alfred's bag.

That did it. They started to argue and fight
and the paint went flying in all directions.

Susie sulked. "I want to go home," she said.
Alfred sulked and said, "I wish you'd never
come in the first place!"

"You're horrible!" exclaimed Susie, stalking off with
her half-finished, messed-up costume.
"Anyway," snorted Alfred, "I can do much better on my own!"

Back at her house, Susie got out her sewing box and the rag bag. "I'll show that Alfred," she muttered, starting to snip and cut furiously.

Later in the day Alfred's mother brought something
to eat. "Where's Susie?" she asked.
"I don't know and I don't care!" Alfred replied.

Next door Susie's mother was surprised. "I thought
you were at Alfred's house," she said.
"I don't like Alfred anymore," said Susie. "I'm
making my costume alone."

Night came and everything was quiet.
Susie's front door opened. A terrible monster appeared.

At the same time Alfred's front door opened.
Out stepped a second terrible monster.

The monsters met under the street lamp.
"HELP! HELP!" squeaked one of them.

"SOMEONE SAVE ME!" squealed the other.

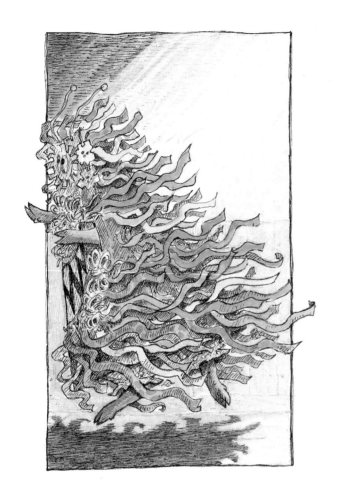 

"Ooh! Aah! EEEEK!" they shrieked wildly.

Suddenly they recognized each other's voices
and stopped and turned.
"Is that really you, Susie? You look fantastic!"
"And you look amazing, Alfred! Let's go
to the party together!"

So they set off.

On the way they were joined by all kinds of weird friends.

At the costume party they had games, lots of
food, and dancing. There was a contest for
the best costume.

Alfred and Susie won first prize together as Mr.
and Mrs. Monster. Their friend Sam came in second.
Nobody knew the little person who came in third.
He must have come from the other side of town.

HELEN CRAIG spent her childhood in the countryside, living in a tiny thatched cottage with no electricity. She worked as a commercial photographer for more than ten years before she began drawing and sculpting. Since her first children's book was published in 1970, she has illustrated numerous books for children, including the Angelina books by Katharine Holabird, the Bonnie Bumble books by Phyllis Root, and *Rosy's Visitors* by Judy Hindley.